POETRY TOWERS

FUTURE VOICES

EDITED BY DAISY JOB

First published in Great Britain in 2023 by:

YoungWriters® Est. 1991

Young Writers
Remus House
Coltsfoot Drive
Peterborough
PE2 9BF
Telephone: 01733 890066
Website: www.youngwriters.co.uk

All Rights Reserved
Book Design by Ashley Janson
© Copyright Contributors 2023
Softback ISBN 978-1-80459-769-9

Printed and bound in the UK by BookPrintingUK
Website: www.bookprintinguk.com
YB0556N

FOREWORD

For Young Writers' latest competition we invited primary school pupils to enroll at a new school, Poetry Towers, where they could let their imaginations roam free.

At Poetry Towers the timetable of subjects on offer is unlimited, so pupils could choose any topic that inspired them and write in any poetry style. We provided free resources including lesson plans, poetry guides and inspiration and examples to help pupils craft a piece of writing they can be proud of.

Here at Young Writers our aim is to encourage creativity in children and to inspire a love of the written word, so it's great to get such an amazing response, with some absolutely fantastic poems. It's important for children to express themselves and a great way to engage them is to allow them to write about what they care about. The result is a varied collection of poems with a range of styles and techniques that showcase their creativity and writing ability.

We'd like to congratulate all the young poets in this anthology, the latest alumni of the Young Writers' academy of poetry and rhyme. We hope this inspires them to continue with their creative writing.

CONTENTS

East Hanningfield CE Primary School, East Hanningfield

Harry Wiltshire (9)	1
Gracie Hill (9)	2
Jude Reater (9)	4
Bonnie-May Crow (11)	6
Harper Ward (9)	7
Eve Patrick (9)	8
Sam Fleming (11)	9
Amelia Sturrock (11)	10
Jhensen Jacques (10)	11
Sofia Hill (9)	12
Reece Smith-Chinnery (10)	13
Jimmy Crow (8)	14
Tamsin Bowler (7)	15
Leia Collins (8)	16
Lily Tompkins (8)	17
Joseph Ravenhill (11)	18
Joseph Roworth (9)	19
Isla Chaston (11)	20
Darcie Reeve (7)	21
Maddison Bowler (9)	22
Oliver Cutts (11)	23
Logan Sexton (10)	24
Ellie Hales (10)	25
Harvey Rostron (10)	26
Daniel Ravenhill (7)	27
James Farrar-Collins (9)	28
Eva Crozier (9)	29
Theodor Taylor (11)	30
Abigail Taylor (8)	31
Edith Fleming (7)	32
Ava-Grace Ingham (10)	33
Rupert Gleadell (8)	34
Olivia Gordon (10)	35
Harry Cutts (8)	36
Jessica Gordon (8)	37
Edie Wheeler (8)	38
Adem Tokgoz (9)	39

Greysbrooke Primary School, Shenstone

Charlotte Cox (8)	40
Cailin Tweedie (7)	42
Henrietta Barry (8)	43
Poppy Horwell (7)	44
Jake Quinn (8)	46
Lola McIntyre (8)	47
George Jacombs-Clarke (8)	48
Scarlett Baynham (8)	49
Mia Taylor (7)	50
Holly Wadsworth (8)	51
Lottie Smith (8)	52
Evie Smart (8)	53
Freddie Strachan (8)	54
Annie Walk (8)	55
Cody Bryant (8)	56
Martha Phillips (8)	57
Martha Withers (8)	58
Georgie Parfitt Turner (8)	59
Jasper James (7)	60
Jonathan Lambert (8)	61
Lucas Browne (7)	62
James Baggott (7)	63
Emily Nolan (7)	64
Phoebe Mbatu (8)	65
Harry Hudson (7)	66
Ronnie Clayton (8)	67
Thomas Nixon (8)	68
Eve Judge (8)	69

Kintore Primary School, Kintore

Lana Findlay (9)	70
Arran Lawson (10)	72
Lyle Duncan (9)	74
Molly Greig (9)	76
Jacob Young (9)	77
Heidi Mottershead (9)	78
Molly Mathieson (10)	79
Robert Cochrane (9)	80
Neave Blackadder (9)	81
Annabelle Tanyous (8)	82
Ellis Munro (9)	83
Madison Wetherly (10)	84
Lukas Soffert (10)	85
Shay Parley (10)	86
Abigail Walker (9)	87
Rory Mathieson (9)	88
Joshua Bartlet (9)	89

Perry Court E-ACT Academy, Hengrove

Grace Chesters (10)	90
Olamide Adedoyin-Onajobi (9)	91
Summerlee Filer (9)	92
Freya Borsay (8)	93
Esme Day (10)	94
Freya Stocks (9)	95
Layla Stuckes (10)	96
Freya Topp (10)	97

Shrewsbury Cathedral Catholic Primary School, Castlefields

Raphie Gutierrez (10)	98
Mitchelle Njini (10)	99
Lena Piechowicz (10)	100

St John's & St Clement's CE Primary, London

Oscar Stirling (8)	101
Omari Shoge (7)	102
Martha McKee (8)	104
Stanley Fagan-Watson (8)	106
Vincent Gilman-Garcia (8)	107
Zinzile Mguni-Jones (7)	108
Esmé Lindsay (7)	109
Amina Ali (7)	110
Isla Gordon (8)	111
Azyrah Quest-Squire (8)	112
Maya Lartey (8)	113

St Luke's Primary School, Cannock

Beatrice Ormand (8)	114
Jay Pham (8)	116
Harrison Thompson (7)	118
Mila Marlow (8)	120
Jaxson Hitchborne (7)	122
Harry Bundonis (7)	124
Lily Smith (8)	126
Spencer Ansell (8)	128
Charlie Brown (8)	130
Jacob Jones (8)	132
Phoebe Spencer (8)	133
Jacob Taylor (8)	134
Jack Wild (8)	136
Alana Rees (8) & Mathilda Maiden (8)	137
Emilia Willis (8)	138
Evie Gough (8)	140
Minnie Degg (7)	141
Megan Geldart (7)	142
Eva Wilkinson (7)	144
Jude Nation (8)	145
Frankie Richards (8)	146
Blake Pritchett (8)	147
Thomas Field (8)	148
Iylah'Rose Wainwright (8)	149
Alfie Piper (7)	150

Darcy Wright (8)	151
Alexandra Hale (8)	152
Carter Wood (8)	153
Ronnie Nixon (8)	154
Layla Mair-Durrant (8)	155
Charlie Cook (7) & Joseph Cox (7)	156
Poppy Bundonis (7)	157
Amber Washington (7)	158
Isabella Nolan (8)	159
Lily Dowell (8)	160
Olivia Vickers (7)	161
Bella Hildich (8)	162
Freddie Hughes (8)	163
Jacob Parsons (8)	164

Watermoor CE Primary School, Cirencester

Anabelle Newbegin (10)	165
Evie Gordon (11)	166
Isla Mills (11)	168

Westwood Prep School, Oldham

Abdullah Al-Hammaad (7)	170
Haleema Khan (9)	171
Muhammed Ahmed (9)	172
Zahra Fatimah (9)	173
Aaisha Kamali (7)	174

Worth Primary School, Poynton

Neva Moores (10)	175
Macie Lawson (10)	176
Zara Wall (9)	177
Molly Griffith (10)	178
Finley Osborne (9)	179
Sebastian Davies (10)	180
Harry Roden (10)	181
Lucy Francis (10)	182
Kye Hindle (10)	183
Betsy Joynson (10)	184
Elliot Murphy-Clarke (10)	185
Isaac Dykes (9)	186
Jack Crabtree (10)	187
Felicity Longden-Boole (10)	188
Rufus Crank (10)	189
Elliot Anderson (10)	190

THE POEMS

POETRY TOWERS - FUTURE VOICES

The Royal Crowning

T he day has arrived
H eir to the throne
E veryone looking their best

K ing Charles takes to the throne
I nside Westminster Abbey
N ot a dry eye in the house
G uards standing proud
S o ready to be crowned

C amilla, his Queen
O n the balcony, they stand
R oyal family by their side
O verlooking the crowd
N ow it's time for Charles to reign
A t 11am the bells will toll
T o tell the world we have a new king
I will wave my flag and shout hooray
O n this most memorable day
N ow it's time to celebrate.

Harry Wiltshire (9)
East Hanningfield CE Primary School, East Hanningfield

Crazy Aisles

Aisle 1
I went to the store and saw
1 duck eating some potato chips!

Aisle 2
I went to the vegetable aisle and saw
2 cats spitting hairballs on everything!

Aisle 3
I went to the sweet aisle and saw
3 dogs gobbling up all the chocolate biscuits!

Aisle 4
I went to the drinks aisle and saw
4 octopuses exploding the fizzy drinks!

Aisle 5
I went to the frozen aisle and saw
5 penguins skating on all the frozen food!

Checkout
I went to the checkout and saw
The zookeeper feeding 6 monkeys!

I was very confused!

Gracie Hill (9)
East Hanningfield CE Primary School, East Hanningfield

The Football Story

Football is my favourite game
The screams and cheers
Make every match the same

Kick-off starts
Your team has to defend
Always in my head, we cannot look
In the end

Here comes Jude. He scored a goal
That run and pass
Deserves his celebration dance.

Those blue and white boots
Never fail
No matter the game
We just sail

Us blue and whites
Are the best team
And one day you'll catch us at Wembley

We're 3-0 up
Taking home the glory
This is the end of my football story.

Jude Reater (9)
East Hanningfield CE Primary School, East Hanningfield

Going On A Dog Walk

One day I went on a long walk,
My dog in my hand and my buddy to talk.
On our way, we met many dogs.
One was an elderly hound, it was saved from the evil pound.
Then we came across a cat, it was a bit of a brat.
Then there was a poodle, he had long fur like noodles.
"Time to head back," I said to my little dog Jack.
"When we get home, you can have a nice juicy bone."
As the sun had now set,
I said to my tired little pet,
"It's time to go to bed
To rest your sleepy head."

Bonnie-May Crow (11)
East Hanningfield CE Primary School, East Hanningfield

Hopes And Dreams

H opes and dreams
O pen, warm hearts
P eople caring for you
E veryone sitting around with you
S cary feelings turning into good feelings

A mazing people around you
N ow's your time to shine
D addy's being your hero

D ogs rule the world
R elieved after you've won
E verywhere is love
A ngels around us
M ummies are there for your worries
S unshine makes the world a good place.

Harper Ward (9)
East Hanningfield CE Primary School, East Hanningfield

Branston Pickle

B ranston is a cheeky pup
R ight in everyone's face
A lways going *ruff ruff*
N ever gonna have a replacement
S till soppy as always
T ime for a walk
O nly one thing, he's still learning to talk
N ice brown good boy

P etted every hour
I t seems like
C razy for attention
K ittens always say no
L ove to play every day
E veryone loves him, he's... our precious pup.

Eve Patrick (9)
East Hanningfield CE Primary School, East Hanningfield

Tottenham, My Team

T ottenham! Tottenham! The crowd chant
O verexcited, hope they score!
T oday's the day, I believe Tottenham will win
T ime after time, I've seen Tottenham lose, but not today!
E ngland has Harry Kane, who is our star scorer and we love him
N ot all hope is lost in Tottenham because they have Son
H opefully, the team will make us happy and rise to the challenge
A lways try to battle to succeed
M agnificently outplaying the opposition!

Sam Fleming (11)
East Hanningfield CE Primary School, East Hanningfield

In The Future

In the future, I'd like to see
Rabbits hopping wild and free.

In the future, I'd like to see
Squirrels not being afraid to come down a tree.

In the future, I'd like to see
Trees not being knocked down full of hundreds of bees.

In the future, I'd like to see
Dolphins swimming against the calm waves of the sea.

In the future, I'd like to see
Millions more stars, more than the eye can see.

Amelia Sturrock (11)
East Hanningfield CE Primary School, East Hanningfield

Memories Of The Queen

Our amazing Queen,
She, as the once ruler of these lands,
Was well known as the longest ruler ever.
Oh great Queen, rest with God high above
the clouds
And watch over us all and
Your son, once a prince, is now a glorious ruler.
Thank you for being so nice to all countries in the
Commonwealth.
You will go down in history as the longest ruler
with a kind heart.
Even though you were 90 you still worked hard
for us all.
So thank you!

Jhensen Jacques (10)
East Hanningfield CE Primary School, East Hanningfield

The Oak Tree

Outside my house
A few steps away
There is an oak tree.
It has soft green leaves
And a thick trunk that looks centuries old.
As I gaze at it from my window
I see the leaves blowing gently in the
evening breeze.
Everything is very quiet and peaceful.
I can only hear the birds chirping
And the dogs barking in the distance.
And I think to myself
How wonderful and special the oak tree is.

Sofia Hill (9)
East Hanningfield CE Primary School, East Hanningfield

Football

I love football
It's my favourite sport
I support Tottenham
They are my favourite team

One minute I'm happy
With Kane and Son
Next min I'm crying
With the poor team show
Some skills are amazing
Then there's VAR

But I will always love football
And Tottenham through and through
For they are my team
And it's a sport I just love.

Reece Smith-Chinnery (10)
East Hanningfield CE Primary School, East Hanningfield

Jammy Jimmy

Jammy Jimmy was fast,
He never let anybody past,
But one day he missed,
The fans hissed.
It was offside,
Everyone cried!
The whistle blew for half-time,
The fans exclaimed, "What a crime!"
A small boy started to sing,
"Come on, Jim, let's get a win."
Jimmy ran out quick
And dribbled past Rick,
He scored a goal
Then the trophy he stole.

Jimmy Crow (8)
East Hanningfield CE Primary School, East Hanningfield

My Hero, Messi

Messi started playing football at the age of four
Now a five-time winner at the Ballon d'Or
A football superstar, he wears a 30 on his back
A golden left foot always in attack
Sixty-eight goals in total for Argentina
133 million followers - sell-out arena!
Was teased for being small with a nickname
of 'Titch'
But this did not stop him, now he is super rich.

Tamsin Bowler (7)
East Hanningfield CE Primary School, East Hanningfield

The Ocean Blue

Many fish live in the water
Sharks and even clapping seals
When I woke up I went to the beach
And I saw a lot of fish to eat
Do you think the ocean is blue
Dark and deep down in the blue?
Time to see what fish there are
Clownfish and eels, oysters with pearls too
When I got up from the sea I saw some otters
That's really rare, I thought to myself.

Leia Collins (8)
East Hanningfield CE Primary School, East Hanningfield

I Love Cats

I love cats

L ong or short haired cats, I don't mind
O bviously very mischievous
V ery cute cats I love so much
E vie, my sister, loves cats too

C ats are one of my favourite animals
A lways with me
T wo cats I used to have, now I have one
S ometimes ferocious but I still love cats.

Lily Tompkins (8)
East Hanningfield CE Primary School, East Hanningfield

Raphael My Tortoise

She is a ray of sunshine.
She's a calming summer breeze.
She's careful when she takes a leaf out of
my hand.
She is a sleepy sloth.
When she wakes up she is as hungry as a hippo!
Her shell is as bumpy as a mound of rocks.
Her skin is tough like dinosaur scales.
Her shell is strong as armoured plates.
That's my Raphael!

Joseph Ravenhill (11)
East Hanningfield CE Primary School, East Hanningfield

POETRY TOWERS - FUTURE VOICES

Lucy, My Lizard

Lucy, my lizard
She is like a wizard
As she makes me happy
Even when I'm blue.

She is fun to study
Small and cuddly.

She is my pet
So far she hasn't
Needed the vet.

She crawls up my arm
But doesn't make me squirm.

I love her to bits
She has me in fits
I love my Lucy.

Joseph Roworth (9)
East Hanningfield CE Primary School, East Hanningfield

Being The Best Big Sister

B rave, to show you are strong!
I con, to behave well so your siblings will copy you.
G enuine to your siblings.

S weet, kind to your siblings.
I ntelligent, to be smart and clever to your siblings.
S uperhero! Most important one of them all is to be a role model to your siblings and be their superhero.

Isla Chaston (11)
East Hanningfield CE Primary School, East Hanningfield

Being A Dancer

D ancing is a wonderful sport that makes you amazing
A cro is a form of gymnastics and makes you super flexible
N othing beats the way dancing makes me feel
C artwheeling all over the stage
E veryone encourages me to be a national champion
R ight now I am dreaming that one day I will be a star!

Darcie Reeve (7)
East Hanningfield CE Primary School, East Hanningfield

Holiday

We've just arrived, for some summer sun,
I can't wait to have some fun!
Trainers off, straight to the beach,
On the way grab an ice cream each.
Take a dip for a swim,
Sun cream on, oily skin.
New friends, blue skies,
Big fat burger, side of fries.
I wish every day was a holiday.

Maddison Bowler (9)
East Hanningfield CE Primary School, East Hanningfield

Greek God Greatness

G reek gods
R uler of the gods
E osphorus is Greek for Lucifer
E ros is Greek for Cupid
K ings of Greece

G ods and goddesses
O ceanus the Titan god
D eadly god of war
S uper gods to live.

Oliver Cutts (11)
East Hanningfield CE Primary School, East Hanningfield

Blaine

My pet is a cat,
She isn't a dog,
Or a slimy frog.

She leaps like a lion
Over great big logs.
She has silky fur
And a comforting purr.

A lizard has scales,
They are not plain.
My pet is a cat
And her name is Blaine.

Logan Sexton (10)
East Hanningfield CE Primary School, East Hanningfield

The River

Haiku poetry

The sun shines brightly,
Twinkling on the pure water,
That's flowing slowly.

It's clear as crystal,
It trickles over the stones,
The water is fresh.

The water dances,
It swirls around lazily,
Supporting much life.

Ellie Hales (10)
East Hanningfield CE Primary School, East Hanningfield

Football Is Me

F ootball is my life,
O ver and over I play,
O n the pitch, I train,
T oday and yesterday,
B ecause I'm a goalie,
A ll the pressure is on me,
L ive, learn, repeat,
L oving football is me.

Harvey Rostron (10)
East Hanningfield CE Primary School, East Hanningfield

Leo

He is as hungry as a horse.
He is as sleepy as a lion.
He is as strong as a whale.
His claws are as sharp as a cat's.
His skin is like a lizard's.
He loves the heat of the sun.
I think his shell is beautiful.
I love my Leo.

Daniel Ravenhill (7)
East Hanningfield CE Primary School, East Hanningfield

The Fire Pit

Haiku poetry

Fire burning bright
The fire pit rising high
Fire quickly grows

Flames dancing in light
The heat burns through anything
Fire slowly dies

The hot heat lives on
Embers continue burning
I am lost in thought.

James Farrar-Collins (9)
East Hanningfield CE Primary School, East Hanningfield

Friends

F riends help you when times are tough
R ead each other stories
I love spending time together
E verlasting fun with you
N ever unhappy
D ay and night fun
S uper happy with you.

Eva Crozier (9)
East Hanningfield CE Primary School, East Hanningfield

Tormented Tim

Rage slithering through his body,
Guilt crackling in his mind,
Sorrow seeping through his veins,
Why is he so tormented?
Nobody knows.
Why is he so angry?
Nobody knows.
How is he still alive?
Nobody knows.

Theodor Taylor (11)
East Hanningfield CE Primary School, East Hanningfield

Crown

C elebrating a special person, the King
R ests on your head for decoration
O n a head if you're a king or a queen
W hen you win something you could wear a crown
N ever make too many crowns.

Abigail Taylor (8)
East Hanningfield CE Primary School, East Hanningfield

A Poem About Me

E xceptional at golf
D elightful with my friends and family
I maginative at making up games
T alented at press ups
H appy when I'm playing with my friends on Fortnite.

Edith Fleming (7)
East Hanningfield CE Primary School, East Hanningfield

Blue-Eyed Sky

My pony is Sky
She is very cute and kind
I love her a lot

    S o cute
    K ind
    Y ou will love her.

Sky is a cob
Sky is 12.3 hands
She is a mare.

Ava-Grace Ingham (10)
East Hanningfield CE Primary School, East Hanningfield

Maizie

M y dog
A lways takes food
I ncredibly cheeky
Z ipped around the countryside
I nfamously noisy
E xtremely loving.

Rupert Gleadell (8)
East Hanningfield CE Primary School, East Hanningfield

Gleam

He's my good boy,
He is looking handsome,
Always good for me.

I love him lots,
Chestnut and super brave,
Love him when cheeky.

Olivia Gordon (10)
East Hanningfield CE Primary School, East Hanningfield

Panda

P erfect cute panda
A dorable things
N ot horrible
D etective Panda to the rescue
A te bamboo minutes ago.

Harry Cutts (8)
East Hanningfield CE Primary School, East Hanningfield

Time For Spring

Rain falls
Horses call
Sun shines
All good signs
Bees buzz
But not near us
Flowers grow
We all know
It's spring.

Jessica Gordon (8)
East Hanningfield CE Primary School, East Hanningfield

Friendship Cinquain

Best friends
Stick together
I will be by your side
Friends cheer you up when you are down
Good times.

Edie Wheeler (8)
East Hanningfield CE Primary School, East Hanningfield

Cats

- **C** ute and cuddly
- **A** lways hungry
- **T** all and timid
- **S** noozing on my bed.

Adem Tokgoz (9)
East Hanningfield CE Primary School, East Hanningfield

My Amazing Dog

My dog is brown and fluffy.
He is my friendly puppy.
He has really sharp teeth
But really small feet.

He is really fast.
Be careful, he's going to come past.
He loves to play.
He's tired at the end of the day.

He is very fun and strong.
He sleeps for very long.
He is really cute.
He eats my black boot.

He has really sharp claws
That can rip down doors.
He is a carnivore so he only eats meat.
Everything he sees he wants to eat.

He is very loud.
He can cause a crowd.
He loves the sea.
He loves barking at trees.

Charlotte Cox (8)
Greysbrooke Primary School, Shenstone

Snow Leopard

S now leopards live in snowy lands
N obody sees them because they blend in with the snow
O nly snow leopards are a type of leopard that's white
W hat can I tell you? I have said a lot already

L eopards are orange but these ones are white
E ats lots of meat like deer and antelope
O n the mountain, they look like snow
P lease look after these animals
A nimals eat grass but not this one
R ead lots of books about this animal
D efend these animals now!

Cailin Tweedie (7)
Greysbrooke Primary School, Shenstone

Snow Leopard

S now leopards are cute
N ever stare a leopard in the eye
O ur snow leopards fight
W e love our snow leopards so stop them from getting hurt

L eopards are orange and black
E at lots of meat
O pposite of stripes
P lease could you go out there and save them?
A lways fun on the grass
R un because it might catch you
D id you know snow leopards can run as fast as a cheetah?

Henrietta Barry (8)
Greysbrooke Primary School, Shenstone

Dog Poem

The cute puppies are white
They are as fast as night
They love balls
And to answer my calls.

Games she has won
And had so much fun
She eats meat
And has four feet

They have a wet nose
And has no toes
They have claws
On their paws

Her tail wags
As quick as flags
She licks my face
And solves a case

She's very cute
And sometimes mute
They clean their plate
Like they play with their mate.

Poppy Horwell (7)
Greysbrooke Primary School, Shenstone

Lions

My lion has orange fur and yellow teeth,
He lives in the jungle and eats meat.

Lots of lions have razor-sharp claws,
He runs around and has lots of wars.

People who see lions would be scared,
Lions are stronger than people so beware.

When he is tired he sleeps under the trees,
People try to shoot him and carefully he can see.

He can dodge the shots because he is fast,
He is very energetic and never comes last.

Jake Quinn (8)
Greysbrooke Primary School, Shenstone

My Piggy

On the day
It was the 3rd of May
The little piggy was out to play
In the mud jumping away

Piggies are never mean
They're like a dream
They're so much like sugar
Way better than butter

They are very nice
But they hate mice
They are only mine
They don't drink wine

Piggies are very cute
They are never on mute
They are very pink
Piggies always have a wink.

Lola McIntyre (8)
Greysbrooke Primary School, Shenstone

Big Black Bear

The big black bear eats big fat fish,
His razor-sharp claws can chop through iron,
And his teeth are as sharp as daggers.
It snoops silently through the wicked woods
And it sleeps and snoozes all through frosty, frozen winter.
Do not cling or cuddle it or you will freshly
And fastly be rapidly ripped to shreds.
The beastly bear is dangerously dangerous
And ghastly, it's vilely vicious.

George Jacombs-Clarke (8)
Greysbrooke Primary School, Shenstone

The White Tiger

W hite fur as soft as wind and breeze
H ears you creeping along the forest floor
I n the jungle, she lurks in the trees
T he wonderful white tiger
E ndangered as a koala

T here in the trees
I nside the dark, scary jungle
G reat, strong tail
E ngaged in killing creatures for food
R oaring noise across the forest floor.

Scarlett Baynham (8)
Greysbrooke Primary School, Shenstone

The Rabbit

They are small and brown
And live in a town
They are cute
But not a brute
They are small
But not a ball

They have cute paws
But no claws
They are small and cute
But sometimes mute
They are brown
And live in a town

They have floppy ears
They have lots of fears
They have a wet nose
But do not pose
They eat carrots
But not parrots.

Mia Taylor (7)
Greysbrooke Primary School, Shenstone

Snow Leopard

S now leopards are cute
N ever wake a baby leopard
O nly leopards have spots
W hat shall I call my baby?

L eopards are orange and black
E ats lots of meat
O pposite of stripes
P lease do not take my snow leopard
A lways runs on grass
R un fast like a cheetah
D id you know snow leopards have fluffy ears?

Holly Wadsworth (8)
Greysbrooke Primary School, Shenstone

Camouflaged Chameleon

C hameleons can change colour whenever they like
H ides in the jungle with its good camouflage
A mongst the trees, they like to climb
M oving through the jungle floor
E melia is the name of the chameleon
L oves to eat lots of juicy bugs
E very day they see other chameleons
O reo is its friend
N ighttime they curl up and sleep.

Lottie Smith (8)
Greysbrooke Primary School, Shenstone

My Cat Called Patch

My cat is fat
I love my cat
My cat is brown
With a spiky head that looks like a crown

He pounces around like a normal cat would
And eats soup and says it's very good
He likes chasing his friend cats
And sometimes goes into caves looking for bats

My cat is funny
He likes using money
He is a scaredy cat
He thinks he is a flying bat.

Evie Smart (8)
Greysbrooke Primary School, Shenstone

Tiger

A fierce tiger would have you for a snack
It has orange and black all over its back
A tiger doesn't walk
It slinks around and stalks

A tiger doesn't fight with its claws
It fights with its jaws
A tiger is big
It likes to eat pigs

Lives in the marsh
It's very harsh
It jumps on a stump
They hunt in the day for their prey.

Freddie Strachan (8)
Greysbrooke Primary School, Shenstone

The Little Wolf

A lovely little wolfy,
So fair and true and fluffy.
But although it is so super duper cute,
You do not know it also is a troublemaker
And a small little brute.

As if you are not aware,
One day you will be cooked unaware!
And you might have guessed the wolf was the chef.
(But he wasn't a good chef because he ate me all up!)

Annie Walk (8)
Greysbrooke Primary School, Shenstone

Bizarre Black Bear

Fur as black as night,
The opposite of light.
Body as big as a tree,
That makes a grown man flee.

See them walk, see them run,
They are just having lots of fun.
Black bears eat salmon,
They also eat gammon.

Bears have huge paws,
With sharp, massive claws.
Black bears are endangered,
So stop putting them in danger.

Cody Bryant (8)
Greysbrooke Primary School, Shenstone

Cheetah

The fast cheetah ran
To find a spot to tan.

She runs fast
In a race, she never comes last.

When she was in danger
She needed a stranger.

She has sharp teeth to eat meat
All the better to eat.

She climbs up high
She is very sly.

The cheetah has yellow fur and black spots
She enjoys to run lots.

Martha Phillips (8)
Greysbrooke Primary School, Shenstone

My Dog

J umps around
A lways happy to see me
C all him on walks
K ind and cuddly

R uns very fast
U ses his tongue to lick the lasagna tray
S mall dog with a big mind
S leeping in my bed at night
E xcited all the time
L ittle dog
L oud bark.

Martha Withers (8)
Greysbrooke Primary School, Shenstone

Snow Leopard

S mall paws...
N ot friendly
O n borders
W hite fur

L and animal
E ats meat
O nly a few of them
P lease don't kill them
A re so cute
R uns really fast
D angerous.

Georgie Parfitt Turner (8)
Greysbrooke Primary School, Shenstone

Turtles

Haiku poetry

It swims in water
They eat seagrass and algae
They have a hard shell.

It has a long tail
They live for one hundred years
They are quite pleasant.

They are very slow
They use four fins for swimming
It mistakes plastic.

Jasper James (7)
Greysbrooke Primary School, Shenstone

The Vicious Tiger

Tigers are big
They love to eat pigs
Springing up on prey
From faraway
It lives in the marsh
It is very harsh
In the day
It catches prey
A fierce tiger would have you for a snack
It has orange and black all over its back.

Jonathan Lambert (8)
Greysbrooke Primary School, Shenstone

The Cheetahs

C an run very fast
H as black spots
E ats meat but no plants
E xcellent at hunting
T ests speed against gazelles
A gile and fragile
H as yellow fur
S prints in the savannah.

Lucas Browne (7)
Greysbrooke Primary School, Shenstone

Lions

Haiku poetry

Sharp claws for hunting
Lions are very fluffy
Lions are big beasts.

Sharp teeth for killing
Lions live on safari
Powerful lions.

Very dangerous
Sharp claws for killing their prey
Lions are quite good.

James Baggott (7)
Greysbrooke Primary School, Shenstone

Big Cat

L ives on land
E very day it hunts
O ver the day it stops hunting
P ounces when it spies prey
A s it hunts it is camouflaged
R azor-sharp teeth
D amage it can do to other animals.

Emily Nolan (7)
Greysbrooke Primary School, Shenstone

Oreo The Cat

Haiku poetry

I like kitty cats
I like Evie's kitty cats
Evie's cats are cute.

They like eating soup
Evie's kitties are silly
They are very cute.

Oreo is cute
He is funny when I visit
I love Oreo.

Phoebe Mbatu (8)
Greysbrooke Primary School, Shenstone

Ancient Egypt

Haiku poetry

There are few houses
Tutankhamun was famous
He was amazing.

Pyramids are huge
The Pyramids of Giza
People are in there.

Egypt has camels
Egypt, a wonderful place
The desert is hot.

Harry Hudson (7)
Greysbrooke Primary School, Shenstone

Tigers

T eeth as sharp as knives
I t lives in the jungle
G oes and hunts every single day
E ats meat and chicken
R azor-sharp claws
S tripes black as night.

Ronnie Clayton (8)
Greysbrooke Primary School, Shenstone

Snake

S ly as can be
N ever gives up on its prey
A nd swallows it whole
K eep away, it might be venomous
E ats mice.

Thomas Nixon (8)
Greysbrooke Primary School, Shenstone

My Cat

My cat has a bad paw
But he still does his part in breaking the law
He is really funny
He never gets muddy.

Eve Judge (8)
Greysbrooke Primary School, Shenstone

Flames

The flames are disruptive and violent.
Like an erupting volcano that can't be controlled.
Like a storm in a glass bottle.
Like a lion's roar that can be heard miles away.
The flames' disrupted, an evil smile makes the earth freeze with fear.

The smoke is as thick as sheep's wool.
The smoke coughs and splutters as it goes up into the Earth's atmosphere.
The smoke's cruel, evil smell of poison and death.
The smoke is a black, deep mystery.

The flames can never be trusted.
You can never trust where they will strike next.
They are cruel and untrustworthy.
The violent flames destroy the forest and devour everything in their path.
The flames push on.
Their violent way.

The flames are terrified of freezing cold water.
The firefighters arrive at the forest.

No one was giving up.
The flames pushed on.
And so did the firefighters.

It was tough
But in the end that felt like forever
The firefighters won.
The smell of defeated flames and smoke never smelt so good before.

Lana Findlay (9)
Kintore Primary School, Kintore

Timmy Bob Mcgregor Junior The Third

The frog went to work at the poisonous power plant
He dashed through the air as fast as a cheetah
Feeling the calm breeze on him

The poisonous sewage was so gooey and gulpy
As poisonous as Venom from Spider-Man 3
Timmy was as cool as a cucumber

But then... *crash!*
The lid of the gulpy, gooey sewage fell off
His body got caught in the sewage
He dashed through the air as fast as Sonic
Timmy was as scared as a man jumping off a cliff

He ran like the Flash
The breeze of him speeding through the air was as cold as Antarctica
A burglar was robbing Timmy with a cunning knife
Timmy fought the burglar off like a lion

He jumped as high as the moon
Bumping into big-eared Yoda
Timmy the Jedi Frog teleported away with his green lightsaber

A few weeks later he was a master of the Force...
Darth Froger showed up like a shooting star
The fighting began
Timmy the Jedi Frog is now a hero like Spider-Man!

Arran Lawson (10)
Kintore Primary School, Kintore

Red Ice

The ice was smooth like butter
The ice was fresh
The ice was as clean as soap
The ice was cold like a lake.

A fight broke out, blood everywhere
Broken jaws, referees trying to stop it
It was brutal
Fighting broke out unexpectedly

The fans were cheering
Welsh players were getting punched in the face
Their blood looked like really red paint
The ice was red, pouring with blood, it was not a nice scene

The people loved it
It was like a crime scene
People were shocked
It was the best fight
All you could hear was punches being thrown right, left and centre

This was the best fight in ice hockey history
People still remember it today

The ice is still red like paint to this day
People are still scarred for life.

Lyle Duncan (9)
Kintore Primary School, Kintore

The Tornado

The wind blew wild, as wild as a bear hunting
The trees were falling down
I was sad
The leaves were happily dancing
All over the grass, I could hear them crunching
The tornado was coming
The tornado was like a roundabout at the park
I heard the rain *drip drop*
The rain stopped
I started to go outside
I smelt the fresh-cut grass
I was touching the grass, it was damp and wet
I could taste the watery rain
My brain was as tired as a marathon runner
I went to my bed, it was as comfortable as a cloud
It was the next morning
The sky was as bright as the colours
I had sizzling Coco Pops
Yum yum
I wanted to go back to bed.

Molly Greig (9)
Kintore Primary School, Kintore

The Midnight Walk

Sitting on a log gazing into the midnight sky
I could feel the smooth grass on my toes
The stars and the galaxy shone down like the sun on a beautiful night
The stars lit the midnight sky like diamonds

The log was as soft as a cushion on my sofa
The trees were rough like stone
The water was clear as ice

The leaves were green and calm like the wind
The knife-sharp grass could cut through butter
The crunchy bark was like crisps

I heard the waterfall crashing
Flowing calmly, I saw a shooting star
It went crashing into the waterfall with a big splash
The frightening water splashed onto me
I was shocked and surprised.

Jacob Young (9)
Kintore Primary School, Kintore

Thunderstorm

The monstrous thunder raged more and more
The fierce lightning crashed and flashed
The gruesome, worried, silver hippo hid under the water for protection
Bash, wurgle, gurgle, bash, wurgle, gurgle
Went the determined thunder and deadly lightning
The thunder roared like a terrifying lion
As horrific as a monkey's laugh
The animals sprinted to shelter
Bang went the enormous thunder
Like a drum pounding
Crash! The gruesome thunder went
Power cables fell as fast as a rhino running for his prey
The leaves floated higher and higher
The lightning demolished buildings
As powerful as a wizard.

Heidi Mottershead (9)
Kintore Primary School, Kintore

Precious Pet Puppy

Buster is the cutest little puppy
Who is really rather lucky.
He lives at my grandma's house
And loves to run and bounce.
In the sun he enjoys to play
With his toys every day.
In his crate, he goes for a nap
But he'd rather sleep on my lap.
Buster is black and white
And he likes to get his tricks right.
He looks at me and wags his tail
Now I know it's time for a trail.
He gets excited for his lunch
And dives straight in, munch, munch, munch.
Buster has lots of wishes
One I think is to give me kisses.
When he snuggles up so tight
You know it's time to go down for the night.

Molly Mathieson (10)
Kintore Primary School, Kintore

The One True Shark

Sharks swim across the golden sand as their fins break into the gold.
Eventually, they head up to the bright glowing coral
The skin is as smooth as a cloud
The fin is as powerful as the jaw
The teeth are as sharp as blades
Coral is growing wildly
The fish swimming in and out of the peaceful reef
It is a rainbow underwater, it sparkles
The fish are swimming as fast as the coral grows
They now swim slower
Into their homes
Sleeping in the dark shadow of the white moon
Then the dawn of playful light covering the dark moon the bright blistering light is as great as The One True Shark.

Robert Cochrane (9)
Kintore Primary School, Kintore

Explosion

It was a dark, gloomy night
The storm moved swiftly past the silver stars.
The town knew that a gloomy storm was coming
The next night the storm started.
Then the explosion exploded with a big *bang!*
And a *thud!*
The bang awoke the city from its dark sleep.
The explosion angrily headed towards the city.
The people screamed in terror because the explosion was going to demolish them all and destroy the city.
The explosion was moving closer to the city.
The people could see that the explosion was the size of a skyscraper…

Neave Blackadder (9)
Kintore Primary School, Kintore

Friends Are Everything

The girls in my class are really cool
They are the best thing about school
Mollie - she is really funny
Maisy likes it when it is sunny
Eilidh thinks crystals are amazing
Miss Leat is really good at hugs and singing
There is Elena - and pandas are her thing
Rachel is the queen of dancing
Charlotte loves a cat to stroke
Georgia likes magic in a wizard's cloak
Chloe has hair like a princess
Siena's name is just the best
It's great to have such good friends
The fun in P4K never ends!

Annabelle Tanyous (8)
Kintore Primary School, Kintore

The Motorway

On a cold Friday night,
Driving on the anxious, busy road,

I can taste the hot and salty McDonald's I ordered,
I can hear angry drivers honking their horns,
As loud as a siren,
I can smell gas coming from the cars,
I can feel the cold leather steering wheel,

My eyes keep going blurry
Because I'm tired
Tired as a sloth

But all of a sudden... *crash.*
All I hear is blaring ambulance sirens,
All I see are bright blue and red flashing lights.

Ellis Munro (9)
Kintore Primary School, Kintore

Forest

I can smell the marshmallow melting slowly over the fire.
The bunnies are as soft and cuddly as my teddies.
I can hear the crackling crunchy leaves beneath my feet.
I can taste the delicious and smooth s'mores in my mouth.
I can feel the heat from the fire on my face.

The trees are taller than a skyscraper.
I can hear the whistling wind whispering to me.
The moon is as big as a mountain.
I can hear the mighty owl hooting at me.
I can smell the pine from the pine trees.

Madison Wetherly (10)
Kintore Primary School, Kintore

The Graceful Waves

The night is a big black cat.

The waves race with the dolphins through the crashing sea
And some waves are whispering as if talking to me.

Some waves shape into me
And the waves smell like salt and vinegar crisps, num-num.

Feeling the waves reminds me of the magic from my heart.

The city behind me glistens like me.
I feel at home because the sea is me.

The waves are my friend to the end of the sea.

Lukas Soffert (10)
Kintore Primary School, Kintore

Edinburgh City

The building towering over you like a tsunami pouncing
And when you look through shiny glass it sparkles and shines like a powerful laser.

The green spaces, free to roam around a magical land for nature
And the wild wind is like a race car in a Formula One race.

The eager birds chirp softly and calmly
Between each tree, drifting like an angel.

The ancient castle sits on the once-angry exploding volcano.

Shay Parley (10)
Kintore Primary School, Kintore

Wretched Waves

The waves are galloping horses
The waves are crackling monsters
The waves are wretched sharks pounding
in the sea
The waves are flying fish jumping in the sea
The waves are a mean tsunami
The waves are flying birds high up in the sky
The sea is a rainbow of colours, teal, blue
and green
I can feel the gushing waves against my feet.

Abigail Walker (9)
Kintore Primary School, Kintore

Best Buddies

Jack is my best friend,
We play happily every break.
We laugh, play games and we love to eat cake.

We both enjoy football
And we tackle each other.
Having loads of fun
It's like having a brother.

Rory Mathieson (9)
Kintore Primary School, Kintore

My New Dog

L ady is my new dog, she is lovely and loyal
A dorable and adventurous, she is fearless and fluffy
D elicate and daring, she is docile and a doddle
Y oung and fun, she is yappy and happy.

Joshua Bartlet (9)
Kintore Primary School, Kintore

Climate Change

C limate change is taking over
L ife is in danger
I want a better future
M any fires going around
A nyone can help stop the pollution
T ime is running out
E very piece of litter that is picked up helps

C an humanity change?
H eat is rising up
A little help is all we need
N ever forget about the animals and plants
G reenhouse gas is also a problem
E arth needs help

In the future, I would like to see some more green.

Grace Chesters (10)
Perry Court E-ACT Academy, Hengrove

What Are We Fighting For?

What are we fighting for?
To chase away the hate,
What are we fighting for?
We should all have mates.
What are we fighting for?
You are so mad,
What are we fighting for?
I make you glad.
What are we fighting for?
You said we are breaking up on a date,
What are we fighting for?
What are you going to say next?
What are we fighting for?
You said we are breaking up in a text,
What are we fighting for?
What are you going to say next?
What are we fighting for
Again?

Olamide Adedoyin-Onajobi (9)
Perry Court E-ACT Academy, Hengrove

The Battle Of The Bands

1x1 is 1
Learning has begun
2x2 is 4
We're higher than before
3x3 is 9
Now I feel divine
4x4 is 16
My classroom is nice and clean
5x5 is 25
What a time to be alive
6x6 is 36
We are now learning all new tricks
7x7 is 49
This poem is all mine
8x8 is 64
Now we're going to next door
9x9 is 81
The battle that was on, we won!
10x10 is 1 and two zeroes
We've reached the end, you're a hero!

Summerlee Filer (9)
Perry Court E-ACT Academy, Hengrove

Friendship

F antastic things will happen
R especting your friend is the most important
I have friendship
E ndless respect
N ice times made with your friends
D oing something nice for them will make you a good friend
S haring your worries with them
H elping them when they need you
I mmerse in friendship with your friends
P ositive things you do help friendship.

Freya Borsay (8)
Perry Court E-ACT Academy, Hengrove

Gem

There once was a girl,
Who found a gem,
She travelled around,
Rock after rock,
Climbing head to toe,
Coming and stretching,
Up and about,
She wondered,
How will she get back home?
No one was there,
Just herself and a gem,
She saw a thing,
In the sky,
A helicopter,
Up in the sky,
Now she can fly.

Esme Day (10)
Perry Court E-ACT Academy, Hengrove

Friendship

To have you as my friend is such a treat
You lift me up when I am down
You're always there for me to greet
You make me smile when I arrive with a frown.

We go together hand in hand
Skipping to have some fun
Maybe we should start a band
And create some music in the sun.

Freya Stocks (9)
Perry Court E-ACT Academy, Hengrove

Ralph, My Dog

R uns like the wind
A cts like a child
L oves his family
P icks up my shoes
H ugs are what he loves.

Layla Stuckes (10)
Perry Court E-ACT Academy, Hengrove

Cats

C ute and fluffy
A dventurous
T o say I love cats, this will do
S hapes and sizes vary.

Freya Topp (10)
Perry Court E-ACT Academy, Hengrove

I Am Human

When I read the news, the selfish, uncaring people say
That I am a bad person.
Am I really a scrounger? A layabout? A bloodsucker?
People call me a monster, or a foolish person
Who takes money as I just ask for help.
"I have no sympathy." "Why would I care?"
Am I really that bad of a person?
No, no! I am human,
Is it that hard to believe? A single world will not hurt me,
They are just absurd people.
So don't tell me I am a layabout, a scrounger or a lounger
Because I am no different to you.
No different than your 'boos'.
So at the end of the day, people will say, "Why would I care?"
But at the end of the day, I will bear the pain
Because I am no different to you.

Raphie Gutierrez (10)
Shrewsbury Cathedral Catholic Primary School, Castlefields

Stop The Fear

After a gruelling journey, they came here.
They came in herds like the plague spreading.
With bombs up their sleeves.
Their words are not like what we say.
The world cannot be looked at another way.

The world can be looked at another way.
They are fleeing away from where they used to stay.
They are not a plague.
They didn't come to invade.
Let them stay
And stop saying what you say.
Instead, let them hear,
You saying,
Stop the fear.

Mitchelle Njini (10)
Shrewsbury Cathedral Catholic Primary School, Castlefields

Change The Story

When I read the news,
'Scrounger' is the word they use.
"It's not our problem,"
Well, then whose?
They call him a scrounger,
While they have nothing left.
They say they're full,
0.24% is a lot, huh?
Put yourself in their shoes,
You will regret those words you used.
They still deserve love,
Everyone deserves love.
We will come to help you.
So don't listen to those saying, "Boo!"
Stop.
And think.
What if it were you?

Lena Piechowicz (10)
Shrewsbury Cathedral Catholic Primary School, Castlefields

Hobbies Galore

Too many hobbies, too many hobbies!
I've got too many hobbies!
My hobbies include:
Basketball, computing, video games,
Lego, Mobilo, K'nex,
Crazy Forts, reading, writing,
Playing at the playground, going to a funfair,
Going on a school trip, going on holiday,
Riding a bike, having a playdate,
Sleepovers, colouring, doing a dot-to-dot,
Playing tag, hide-and-seek, freeze tag
And watching TV.

    H ilarious playdates
    O utstanding homework
    B arbecues
    B all games
    I ncredible igloo designs
    E njoyed holidays
    S uperduper dot-to-dot.

Oscar Stirling (8)
St John's & St Clement's CE Primary, London

Loving Nature

The beauty of nature allows us to live.
The wind, it's blowing, it always is.
It blows up the kites but has always hid.
The sun burns but helps some plants
Like bluebells, sunflowers and other plants like this.
The flowers bloom every summer but start on another.
The rain splashes on the floor
Which makes the puddles you'll find on the floor.
Snow and snowflakes fall down slowly shaping in the sky.
The moon is high, it shines up bright.
A lonely tree, it has no friends
At night it leans into the night.
The trees are happy in the day
The birds lay eggs inside the nests
But in the night the wind starts whistling its favourite tunes
On the whistling way.
The fish glide through the sea.
They always mate in a certain season.

It's so surprising how they live when sharks are storming everywhere.
It's so surprising how nature is so
You should always look out for beautiful things around you.

Omari Shoge (7)
St John's & St Clement's CE Primary, London

Help Our Planet

H urry up and save our plants, our animals and trees
E lephants, rhinos, pandas, and orangutans, save all these
L ove the world but we need to succeed
P oor animals struggling, so help the planet and do a good deed

O rangutans are in danger, it's even bad for us to feel such a failure
U s people are the problem so let's save their precious town
R ainforests are being cut down, these animals don't have a town

P eople, just stop polluting, why can't you put your litter down?
L ions and zebras, save them all because we're really letting them down
A nimals and people's lives are the same, if they were us would we be the same?
N ot enough, not enough, we have to help them so much

E ver, ever, ever again? No, no, no! We will help our planet!
T rees are being destroyed so animals have no joy.

Martha McKee (8)
St John's & St Clement's CE Primary, London

King Of Crystals

K ing of crystals, slowly falling down
I n the cold wind, blowing past
N ice and sparkling in the sun
G iant this one, lying in my hand

O n the floor now, slipped off my hand
F ell down from a dark dark cloud

C rystal clear, not foggy at all
R ocky? No! No bumps at all
Y achts are sailing, they fall on the mast
S ilent these are, invisible too
T inkling down from the sky it goes
A nd they are so beautiful you could faint
L ines are brilliant on these things
S nowflakes! Snowflakes! Did you know?

Stanley Fagan-Watson (8)
St John's & St Clement's CE Primary, London

Too Many Hobbies

So I have lots of hobbies.
I wonder if you do?
Okay, I will start by telling you about my hobbies:
Okay, hmm...
I like football, basketball,
TV, video games, reading,
Drawing, writing, playing mini golf,
Bouncy castle, slides, typing
And that's it.
That's a lot of hobbies, right?

H appy and fun
O utstanding sports
B est time waster
B est for playing with friends
I ce skating is a hobby
E xciting hobbies are fun
S uper good at everything!

Vincent Gilman-Garcia (8)
St John's & St Clement's CE Primary, London

Gymnastics Champ

When I grow up I want to be amazing
in gymnastics.
I want to be the best I can be,
My favourite part is the competition.
I have recently won gold and stuck an aerial.
I want to achieve a roundoff flick double tuck
and pike.
When I grow up I want to be the best.
I love my gymnastics because I love getting
dizzy in tricks and stuff.
I want to be the best I can be.

Zinzile Mguni-Jones (7)
St John's & St Clement's CE Primary, London

Why Do We Learn?

Why do we learn every day?
Who will teach on the holidays?
When will I stop or will I learn forever
And what can I do to help me learn more?
Learning is hard but it's also fun.
I hope I learn forevermore.
You can learn from play or you can learn from work.
So many questions to answer which is why we learn!

Esmé Lindsay (7)
St John's & St Clement's CE Primary, London

Poems

P eople write lots of poems, poems can be about anything
O ver there is a girl writing a poem, I wonder what it's about
E lephants? Could be. Hmm, I don't know, well
M aybe it's about food. Let me go and ask her... Hello...
S ee how poems are amazing.

Amina Ali (7)
St John's & St Clement's CE Primary, London

Panic Panda

Once when I was younger, I fell out of a tree,
I landed on my tummy and bounced from knee to knee,
But then when I was older,
I climbed up the very same tree as before,
And I did not fall down and I stayed in there forevermore.

Isla Gordon (8)
St John's & St Clement's CE Primary, London

I Love Calmness

I love maths, I love maths,
I love my mum, I love my mum,
I love calmness, I love calmness,
I love nature, I love nature, I love nature,
I love writing, I love writing, I love writing.

Azyrah Quest-Squire (8)
St John's & St Clement's CE Primary, London

Love

L ove everyone
O ver the planet, love can be spread
V alentine's Day is a day for love
E ven if people don't love you love them back.

Maya Lartey (8)
St John's & St Clement's CE Primary, London

The River

The start of a river is called the source,
And then it goes off to start its course.
The waterfall calls children to come and play,
They love it so much they want to stay.

Tributaries are like little streams,
And when they join together they feel like they're in a dream.
They went downhill like a windmill,
And had a good view on the hill.

The meander's reflections glow as they slowly flow,
When waving to the sea that is slow.
The meander twists,
Before it goes through mists.

The estuary is flowing into the slowing end of the south,
On its way to the great big mouth,
As it runs down like a stream,
It is as big and straight like a wooden beam.

The mouth is flowing into the bellowing end of the river,
This is where it starts to shimmer,
This is the end of all the flow,
Now it can finally let the river go.

Beatrice Ormand (8)
St Luke's Primary School, Cannock

Beautiful River

The sparkling water and beauty of spring,
The modern clean water near the astonishing mountain.
The open-wide source,
The trees were surrounding me as I thought the seas were surrounding me too.

The stream hisses like a snake and nature whistles,
The merry birds tweet a peaceful song to me,
The river flows like a professional dancer meandering,
We were approaching the delta until we
saw shelter.

As the winding and meandering river flowed,
Through the ocean breeze,
The river was pure and clean and flowed with a meandering slither,
As the water got faster it formed into a team
And bubbled more and more until it shot up like a blaster.

It finally stopped curving,

The sun shone bright, it began to glisten,
The shine on the mouth of the river,
Looked like it started to cool down and shiver.

Jay Pham (8)
St Luke's Primary School, Cannock

The River

The source comes down a mountain,
It's a bit like a fountain.
It trickles down the mountain very fast,
It's extremely vast.

The tributaries run water into the river,
When you get in you will shiver,
The river flow is extremely slow,
It has an amazing flow.

As the river twists and turns, a meander starts,
Oxbow lakes cut it off and take a different part,
It's extremely narrow,
The flow is like a bow and arrow.

The beauty of a river is amazing as it reflects on me,
The estuary runs water into the sea,
It's like it's going to flee,
It dances like it's in glee.

Now the silky river is done it's run into the sea,
It was like a racer going to flee,
Now all the water from a little drop has created a colossal, deep river.

Harrison Thompson (7)
St Luke's Primary School, Cannock

The River

The river appears as a beautiful stream,
This stream is jewellery gleam,
The majestic river flows,
As the flashing wind blows.

Watch the tributaries walk into the river,
It is as fast as Flash when it quivers,
The tributaries smile when they join the stream,
It is like a magical dream.

The meander curls like a fossil as it's twirling,
This meander is a worm swirling,
This is a scaly snake,
Then it causes an oxbow lake.

The clear water mixes with the river,
If you hop into the river it will give you a shiver.
I love this ice bath stream,
The river is like my favourite dream.

This is the end of the river, a mouth,
This mouth is down south.

This is the most amazing stream,
But the stream ran into the hot sea and created steam.

Mila Marlow (8)
St Luke's Primary School, Cannock

The River

The start of a river is called a source,
When it gets going it starts a course.
The river is going very fast,
It went down in a blast.

All the tributaries make the river larger,
On there, you might see a big, colourful barger.
The tributary was going very slow,
It went down a hill and that's when it got a flow.

The meander has formed an oxbow lake,
People are getting the ground ready with a rake.
The meander set off the floodplain,
It flooded as fast as a speedy train.

The big, clean estuary,
Is the river's destiny.
When the river met the ocean of salt,
A boat had a massive fault.

To get to the mouth,
You need to go south.
Fish are working as a team,
People say the mouth is large as it does seem.

Jaxson Hitchborne (7)
St Luke's Primary School, Cannock

The River

The start of the river is called a source,
When it gets going it goes into a course.
The meander has formed a straight oxbow lake,
The meander is a curly snake.

When the river gets larger,
You might see a beautiful barger.
It is getting closer to the salty, blue sea,
Lots of people were on a canoe including me.

When the tributaries join they are fast,
Now it goes down in a blast.
When the tributaries join it will slither,
Down the turquoise river.

The water is,
Getting shorter.
It is mixing with the salt,
People were watching a dolphin do a somersault.

You need to go south,
To get to the mouth.

The water is freezing,
On the beach, lots of people were sneezing.

Harry Bundonis (7)
St Luke's Primary School, Cannock

The River

The clear blue river starts as a waterfall,
It's got hydrating water for all.
As the source gets bigger it turns to a stream.
Then on a stream, I had a dream.

As the tributaries flow, I saw a glow.
Watch the tributaries flow so slow, watch
them put on a show.
In the past, I walked fast.
In the past, I was last.

The river twists in the midnight sky.
Watching its prey as the moonlight passes by.
Watch the stream dance in the night.
Feel the water so light.

The river continues to its final,
Although it's only water.
The water becomes a daughter,
But now I'm a sorter.

To get to the mouth,
Go to the south.
I had a dream on the sea.
It was about me.

Lily Smith (8)
St Luke's Primary School, Cannock

The River

The source of the river starts from a tall mountain.
It's a bit like a running, speedy fountain,
It jogs down a hill very fast,
It's extremely vast.

The tributaries run water into the river,
When you jump in there, you will shiver,
The river flow is extremely, crazily slow,
It digs in the ground low.

It meanders like a slithering, long snake,
But is a speedy lake,
It will always bend,
Before the end.

The estuary is where it will mix in the stream,
So it might steam,
It mixes together,
And it's there forever.

The end is the mouth,
And it's always south

It goes to the sea,
And that's the end of the amazing journey!

Spencer Ansell (8)
St Luke's Primary School, Cannock

The River

The start of the river is called a source,
Something came to drink the river water,
it could be a horse.
Look at that lovely, clean waterfall,
It's water for all.

So many tributaries join way too fast,
But that is in the past.
If you go in the stream,
It will make you scream.

The river is the cloudy blue sky,
The river flows like a flying bird passing by.
The vast snake hissed,
Whilst the river did a twist.

At daybreak, the estuary water is like the water in the south,
The estuary finally reached the mouth,
This is a river,
And it makes you shiver.

The sea laughed,
As the ocean thrashed.
The heat,
Makes your heart beat.

Charlie Brown (8)
St Luke's Primary School, Cannock

The Running River

As I woke up the birds were starting to sing,
As I looked out of the window it was spring.
As the water was cascading down the stream,
It gave me an amazing, awesome dream.

The fantastic river was going upstream as it was bubbling,
The blue, sapphire river was dribbling.
The snake in the water had a slither,
The scaly snake was going downstream in the river.

The river was amazing to watch because of the flow,
The river was so cool because it had a glow.
Soon it flowed into the ocean,
The water had a motion.

The refreshing water had a dream,
The water was going downstream.
The awesome beauty went downstream,
The beautiful stream had a dream.

Jacob Jones (8)
St Luke's Primary School, Cannock

The River

The start of a wide river is the source,
And it goes as fast as a horse!
If you go on a light blue canoe down the stream,
You will let out a time-looping scream!

Tributaries are small,
But they can make the vast river tall.
It is clean like cream,
And because of the tributaries, it's a stream.

The river is a twisting vein going down the hill,
And when it turns too much it will spill.
When the salt and fresh water mix it makes
an estuary,
At this point, it has almost reached its destiny.

If you are travelling down south,
You will find the mouth.
It has reached the end of its trip,
It is now going to the sea for a dip.

Phoebe Spencer (8)
St Luke's Primary School, Cannock

The River

This is the start of a river called the source,
This is the start of its course.
The source of the river has a waterfall,
It is as big as a cliff fall.

The tributaries are little streams,
They are so fast they sound like screams.
The tributaries have a great flow,
Because they're going to go.

The shining, meandering river,
Is a giant shimmer.
The meandering river is very fast,
As it flows speedily past.

Its journey is a lot shorter,
Like as much as a quarter.
It has a good flow,
It's going so slow.

The mouth smiled at the sea,
I thought it smiled at me.

So this is the end,
Goodbye, my good friend.

Jacob Taylor (8)
St Luke's Primary School, Cannock

The Journey Of A River

And so it all starts,
Right at the beginning part.
The fish are like a blue ribbon that decorates the land,
And the trees sway and swerve as they fanned.

As the bubbling lake passes the giant Eiger,
It secretly roars like a tiger.
The lake passes by as it takes its course,
The source slowly goes as it takes the path and follows the horse.

The small river meanders through forest flowers,
It ends as it glides through the river's powers.
Then it flows and lulls the birds to sleep,
As the fur-coated bears begin to creep.

Soon it flows into the ocean,
The water has motion.
The water is moving,
As it is so cooling.

Jack Wild (8)
St Luke's Primary School, Cannock

The Lavender River

The fresh water swayed down the glistening stream,
The fresh smell of nature was like a dream.
Sound of the calming birds make soothing music in the spring,
When you see beautiful bluebirds calmly sing.

The sapphire blue ribbon decorates the mint green land,
As it feeds nature and gives God a helping hand.
The bubbling water flowing through when it was velvet blue,
As it cascades down the jagged mountains with my canoe.

Then the river was cascading down and fell,
It was a colossal splash that could sound like a bell.
We can see the huge mouth so the last part,
It was the sea that looked like a jam tart.

Alana Rees (8) & Mathilda Maiden (8)
St Luke's Primary School, Cannock

The River

As the river began at the source,
The majestic river was an obstacle course.
As the river went down the stream,
It was like a very nice dream.

As the tributaries joined the river,
When it went down we saw it slither.
As we jumped in the river,
Me and my friends started to shiver.

As we saw meanders twirl it was very mean,
When it went past we were very keen.
As it went past,
It was very fast.

As I saw an estuary,
It commanded my destiny.
As I saw the sea,
It saw me.

As I saw the river mouth,
It was going down south.

As I saw the beautiful sea,
My friend was looking at me.

Emilia Willis (8)
St Luke's Primary School, Cannock

The River

This is the start of a river and it's called a source,
But this is where it begins its graceful course.
The river went downhill,
As fast as a windmill.

This is a meander but it was as twirly as a worm,
And every touch it is a perm.
The river water took another route because
it is solo,
But it was as soft as a blanket like a flow.

As the river water and the seawater connect,
They were both hugging as they protect,
As it flows into the colossal river past,
The sea was a big, huge blast!

As they mixed the sea was massive but it was
a river!
And it danced on the dancefloor like a shimmer.

Evie Gough (8)
St Luke's Primary School, Cannock

Degg's River

The bubbling river went anxiously past the big delta,
Which was badly close to the small shelter.
The crashing, whooshing and splashing river went with the flow,
Into the spring where people would sing as he went very low.

The bubbling, glistening and shining river wanted to fly,
In the big, blue and clean, sparkling sky.
Under the summer sun, it is really warm,
But I think there's gonna be a little storm.

Glistening water trickles on my warm head,
Trickle, drip, drop, my canoe calmly goes past which feels like a bed.
The blue ribbon decorated the land,
Giving people a helping hand.

Minnie Degg (7)
St Luke's Primary School, Cannock

The River

As the river began at the source,
The shiny river was on an obstacle course,
As the river went down the stream,
It was like a Roblox meme.

As the tributaries join we see the river,
As it goes down we see it slither.
Tributaries are small,
But they make the river very tall.

I walked to the meander, I loved its flow,
It was slow.
I watched it turn,
I saw it learn.

I watched an estuary go by,
It was fun,
In a hot, hot sun,
I saw an estuary,
It was my destiny.

I visited the mouth,
So I walked south.
I loved it there,
I asked to stare.

Megan Geldart (7)
St Luke's Primary School, Cannock

The River

The river starts as a waterfall.
It's got hydrating fresh water for all.
As the source gets bigger it turns to steam.
Then on a stream, I had a dream.

As the tributaries flow I saw a glow.
The tributaries flow so slow
Then put on a show.
In the past one was fast.
In the past one was last.

The fresh glistening meander was
Beginning to swirl and dance.

As the meander was twirling like a snake
On the meander, I ate some steak.
The estuary got together, the weather got heavy.
As the weather gets heavier it gets littler each time
And that's how it gets littler.

Eva Wilkinson (7)
St Luke's Primary School, Cannock

The River

This is the start of the river, it is called the powerful source,
This is the start of the river's course,
The source of the river is a waterfall,
This is where the river falls.

Tributaries join the stream,
It is that beautiful it feels like a dream.
Tributaries have a flow,
Even though it is super slow.

The river runs like a snake,
The meander turns into a big, long lake.
It swims and runs for a while,
Even though it feels like a mile.

The estuary has a collided flow,
It is super massively slow.
It collides with colour,
It is light blue in the summer.

Jude Nation (8)
St Luke's Primary School, Cannock

The River

The start of the river is called the source,
And then it goes off to start its course.
The waterfall calls children to come and play,
They love it so much they want to stay.

Tributaries are like little streams,
And when they join together they feel like they're in a dream.
They went downhill,
Like a windmill.

The meander is fast,
But it can go vast.
When you get into the river,
It will make you want to shiver.

The ocean-blue water flows into the sea,
And then it squirts water all over me.
Finally, I can see,
A giant wave calls me.

Frankie Richards (8)
St Luke's Primary School, Cannock

The Mighty River's Journey

The sky-blue river glistened in the sunshine,
It went through the forest and past the Rhine.
The water vein ran as a deer passed by,
Suddenly the deer sprinted away, but why?

The water line rushed through a field of flowers,
It went past ancient ruins and towers.
It passed another field of flowers that had a beautiful scent,
Through the land, it went.

The sea was not far away as the river said goodbye,
As it left its animal friend it was shy.
It got extremely close to the mouth,
Finally, the sea swallowed the river so now with the sea it was heading south.

Blake Pritchett (8)
St Luke's Primary School, Cannock

The Beauty Of A River

Bubbling water flowed from a spring,
The soothing sound of the many birds singing.
The sparkling water and the beauty of spring,
The modern clean water, I could see the reflection of the bees.

As the winding and meandering river,
Flowed through the breeze with a meandering slither.
As the meandering river got faster,
It formed a team and then a wave appeared, it shot water like a blaster.

It finally stopped curving and the sun shone,
When it started to go dark the sun had gone.
We got to the mouth of the river,
It slowly started to coldly shiver.

Thomas Field (8)
St Luke's Primary School, Cannock

A River Stream Lake

The cool stream started off slow,
Then up with a steady flow.
The stream bubbled as it went down the hill,
Near the end, it started to chill.

The chirping birds were by the picturesque stream,
Singing their beautiful chorus, it sounded like
a dream.
The blue ribbon decorated the land,
As it gave God a helping hand.

The bubbling water and natural springs,
The soaring of the birds' wings.
A meander, as it flowed through a field full of
lavender.

The bubbling water and natural springs,
The soaring of the birds' wings.

Iylah'Rose Wainwright (8)
St Luke's Primary School, Cannock

The Journey Of A River

The sky, the river glistened in the sunshine,
It went through the forest and the Rhine.
The water vein ran past a deer,
Suddenly it moved away, but why?

The birds sang a song that I could hear,
They sang louder as they got near.
Bubbling hot springs fizzed and popped,
The river went past the springs until it dropped.

The sea was not far away, as the river said goodbye,
As it left its animal friends it would be alone, it was shy.
It got extremely close to the mouth,
Finally, the sea swallowed, now it was heading to the sea south.

Alfie Piper (7)
St Luke's Primary School, Cannock

Darcy's River

The cool stream starts off slow,
Then speeds up with a steady flow.
The stream bubbles as it goes down the hill,
But near the bottom, it starts to chill.

The chirping birds are picturesque streams,
Singing their beautiful chorus, it sounds like a dream.
The blue ribbon decorates the land,
As it feeds nature and gives God a helping hand.

The bubbling water and natural springs,
The soaring of birds' wings.
The river is following a meander,
As it flows through a field of lavender.

Darcy Wright (8)
St Luke's Primary School, Cannock

The River

The start of a river is called the source,
And it now begins its course.
The sky-blue stream twisted and turned in the past,
The river went fast.

The wavy stream is as small as a mouse, now it is big,
But it is dirty with fish and twigs,
The river is huge, big, not small or tall,
The people always come to the river all.

The river meandered in the past,
At the same time, there was a mast,
On the pirate ship in the ocean,
On the pirate ship, there was a potion.

Alexandra Hale (8)
St Luke's Primary School, Cannock

Water's Ways

I could hear the water bubbling,
I realised it was doubling.
The sky was blue and clear,
The birds' chorus I could hear.

The river has a source,
That flows in a gentle course.
The water was pure sapphire blue,
As I approached and meandered in my canoe.

I saw the gentle breeze,
Shake the trees.
The blue ribbon decorates the land,
Giving God a helping hand.

The twirling lake,
Meandered like a snake.
The blue water waved,
Dazzled and dazed.

Carter Wood (8)
St Luke's Primary School, Cannock

The Sparkling River

The sparkling water was pouring,
When the big Eiger was snoring.
The curving river when it was fast,
It was becoming a big ghost.

When it was loud with a cloud in a beautiful sky it was the ocean,
Then suddenly there was something blue with some motion.
The beautiful river was sky-blue,
As I was sleeping in my canoe.

As the winding river gave me a dream,
Maybe it was something like a stream.
The bubbling water was deep,
Like there was something to keep.

Ronnie Nixon (8)
St Luke's Primary School, Cannock

The River

The clear sapphire river flows fast,
Through the waterfall as it goes past.
As the beautiful birds sang,
All the birds started to make a gang.

The blue ribbon decorates the land,
As it feels nature and gives God a hand.
The sky is as blue as an ocean,
It smells as divine as a potion.

The source of a glistening river,
Starts with a little bit of a shiver.
The smooth calming stream flows,
And there is an emerald field covered with snow.

Layla Mair-Durrant (8)
St Luke's Primary School, Cannock

River Journey

The glistening stream is as bright as the sun,
The beginning of the journey has just begun.
The bottom of the mountain head,
It turns big at the river bed.

The nice, gentle, relaxing flow,
In the reflected glow.
The glorious, sapphire blue,
As the crazy river pushed the canoe.

The brilliant river looks like it is invisible and clear,
As the river sped up you could hear.
The slow, clear crystal ocean,
Bubbling, buzzing, wavy motion.

Charlie Cook (7) & Joseph Cox (7)
St Luke's Primary School, Cannock

The Clear River

A bubbling spring was calm and flowing
As the birds started to sing when it started snowing
As the river flowed down the mountainside
The fish swam and the swans did glide.

The water was soft and kind, it was clear
It was happy, it was streams I could hear
It was like a fast snake
Then it was a calm lake.

It was a glistening blue sky
I could see the birds calmly fly
The dipper was on the river
As the river started to quiver.

Poppy Bundonis (7)
St Luke's Primary School, Cannock

Amber's Bubbling Lake

A bubbling spring was calm and flowing,
As the birds started to sing and it started snowing.
As the river flowed down the mountainside,
The fish swam and the calm swans did glide.

The water was soft and kind, it was clear,
It was happy, it was blue streams I could hear.
It was like a mad, fast snake,
Then it was a calm lake.

It was a glistening blue sky,
I could see the birds fly.
I love the river,
It gave me a shiver.

Amber Washington (7)
St Luke's Primary School, Cannock

The Journey Of A River

The clear sapphire river flowed fast,
Through the waterfall as it went past.
As the beautiful birds sang,
All the birds started a gang.

The source of a calming river,
Started with little of a shiver.
The smooth calming stream flowed,
And there was an emerald field covered with snow.

The hooting birds sang with a hoot,
Flapping their wings like a flute.
A gang of sleeping lions' paws,
As I could hear a lion snore.

Isabella Nolan (8)
St Luke's Primary School, Cannock

The River

The start of a river is called the source,
And it goes as fast as a horse!
If you go on a canoe down the stream,
You will hear a loud scream!

Tributaries are small,
But can make the river tall,
It is so clean like cream,
It also has tributaries so it is a stream.

The meanders are twisting and twirling like a gymnast,
So we can't see it go past,
And it will gracefully grow,
Then it will go with the flow.

Lily Dowell (8)
St Luke's Primary School, Cannock

The Lavender River

The peaceful, calm river started to meander,
And it also had a smell that was lavender.
When I went through the city in a storm,
It was surprisingly warm.

As the water was as bright as the sun,
The journey had begun.
As the bubbling water began to flow,
It also started to snow.

The sky was so blue and clear,
All of the birds I could hear.
Bubbling water and natural spring,
As I heard the amazing birds sing.

Olivia Vickers (7)
St Luke's Primary School, Cannock

The River

The source of the river flowed as slowly as
a slug going past.
As the last star remained the source went
downhill like a leopard so fast.

The tributaries were in the ground so slow.
The tributaries were the same speed as a sloth
would go if they were in the trees, they would flow.
The meander is a lake, it slithered like a
sparkling snake.

As the sun shone across the ocean
The ocean was a glistening-like motion.

Bella Hildich (8)
St Luke's Primary School, Cannock

The River

The river starts in a mountain up high
And this is where it will lie.
The river is long
It has a mouth but it doesn't have a tongue.

I have a flow that is extremely slow.
The river has a nice flow.
It is fast
But it is not in the past.

The sparkling meander begins to twirl,
It glows and flows into a swirl.
There is a lot of mist.
The river can twist.

Freddie Hughes (8)
St Luke's Primary School, Cannock

The River

The opening of a river is called a source,
This is where it starts its obstacle course.
As the tributaries found the massive river it started to glow.
The massive river was very slow.

The river slithered like a snake,
This is like a lake,
The river is as fast as a bike,
In the river, you might find a broken trike.

Jacob Parsons (8)
St Luke's Primary School, Cannock

Life Is Like A Flower

Life is like a flower.
It grows, spreads and dies,
Some are quicker than others.

Some lives are big, bold and brave,
Like a sunflower reaching to the sky.

Some are perhaps a black iris,
Small and quiet,
Lonely and unnoticeable.

Whereas others might be a simple daisy,
Normal and common but still beautiful.
However, throughout our lives,
We will change the flowers,
It's a part of our lives.
As well as being picked.

Anabelle Newbegin (10)
Watermoor CE Primary School, Cirencester

Bringing Colour Back To A Black And White World

Lime green leaves uncurling in the wind ready to begin a new day,
Grass shining in the morning sunrise, yawns being spread around,
Buds waiting quietly and patiently for their time to bloom,
The different shades of green start to fill my plain canvas.

Radiant red berries ready to be eaten by ravenous birds,
Beautiful roses swaying in the calm breeze filling the air with their perfume,
Ladybugs hide in their favourite leaves, hoping they don't attract curious eyes.

The unique yellow sunflowers bring smiles and light to our days,
Busy bees making our beloved honey,

The sun shone, standing out in the darkness of the shade.

These colours are so important to our world,
Sometimes we forget how lucky we are that our world isn't black and white,
Colours make us feel emotions we've never felt before,
So remember to keep your head up and embrace the glory of colour.

Evie Gordon (11)
Watermoor CE Primary School, Cirencester

The Feast Of The Blue Wolf

The Northern Lights danced gracefully in the pale violet sky, last night.
The small grey mice scurried to and fro in the silver moon's light.
The wolf with blue fur lay in the grass, lying, waiting.

She should have been with her pack, last night.
After all, wolves usually hunt in small groups.
Not this wolf though, as she lay, waiting.

Before long, a moose went into the clearing, he was in danger, last night.
The wolf narrowed its emerald eyes, looking through the long grass.
Then with all her might, the wolf pounced, no longer lying, waiting.

After her wonderful feast, the wolf trekked up to her den, last night.
She eventually made it to the cave, leaving snowy footprints in her wake.

One hour later, she was asleep, lying, waiting.
Waiting for the morning's sunrise.

Isla Mills (11)
Watermoor CE Primary School, Cirencester

What Is It?

In a meadow green, where flowers bloom,
Hops a little creature with fluffy fur,
With ears so long and eyes so bright,
It scurries around in the pale moonlight.

Its fur is soft, as white as snow,
It's nimble and quick, with a cute little nose.
It nibbles on carrots, its favourite treat,
With a twitch of its nose, it's hard to beat.
In a burrow underground it makes its home.
What is it?
Guess what it is.

Answer: A rabbit.

Abdullah Al-Hammaad (7)
Westwood Prep School, Oldham

Candy Cottage

C andy is delicious
A mazing colours everywhere
N ice to look at
D elicious to eat
Y ummy in my tummy

C ottage made of carrot cake
O h so yummy
T asty chocolate cakes
T errific colours around the cottage
A dventurous to fly to candy mountain
G orgeous to look at cotton candy trees
E normous swirly whirly lollipops.

Haleema Khan (9)
Westwood Prep School, Oldham

Poem Powers

P oem books I love
O h please can I have one? I'll be as good as Sahabah
E very time you say no
M um, I have enough money

P lease
O h please
W hy not get a diary?
E ntries to diaries are as hard as memorising a 500-page book
R acing cars, I could get a severe injury
S o give me a poem book.

Muhammed Ahmed (9)
Westwood Prep School, Oldham

What Am I?

I need a stick to hold me up.
I sometimes find myself in sticky situations.
The more you use me the smaller I get.
I come in every colour of the rainbow.
Usually, I am round,
Sometimes there is a surprise in the middle.
You can't enjoy me unless you suck me.
What am I?

Answer: A lollipop.

Zahra Fatimah (9)
Westwood Prep School, Oldham

All About SF

SF is kind, helpful, she makes me smile
She plays with me
She is very kind to people who are sad
SF, you are funny all the time
I feel so amazed
I like you so much
Thank you for doing this.

Aaisha Kamali (7)
Westwood Prep School, Oldham

Rainforest Animals

Hear the rain in the rainforest, the sun shining from behind the trees.
The birds flapped their colourful wings, flying into the breeze.
Now the reptile slithers out from its dark, damp cave,
The snake fancies a mouse today as that is its absolute fave.
Here comes the monkey swinging from tree to tree,
It stops at a sloping branch and goes down shouting wee!
Look over there at that beautiful bird,
You might scare it so don't say a word.
Now it's flying to its nest,
It's a place where all birds like to rest.
Finally, the moon rises and the day is done
Sadly it's the end of all our fun.
The animals are asleep curled up in their beds,
All dreaming sleepily and resting their heads.

Neva Moores (10)
Worth Primary School, Poynton

Strange Memory

I remember something that happened to me
Long ago in two thousand and three
I was only four and it was in July
When I went to the zoo and I started to cry
My mum said, "What's the matter?"
And I said, "Look at that monster."
She started to laugh and then looked at
me seriously
I pointed it out and then scowled at it deviously
I started to smirk and it did the same
My mum pulled y hand and over it came
I managed to get away and we started to fight
And it went on and on and on all through the night
It was all over the news, well that's what I reckon
And all of a sudden we stopped for a second
And that's the story of how a monster became
my best friend!

Macie Lawson (10)
Worth Primary School, Poynton

My Pet Tree Who Hates His Leaves

My pet tree hates its leaves,
But I don't know why.
He groans and moans all day and night.
But days came by and months came by
And autumn came,
The poor leaves cried,
"Oh no, oh no, sorry but now it's time, goodbye."
Except my tree felt bad and then lightning struck.
"Stay with me, friend," shouted my tree.
I screamed in shock.
"My pet tree is magical," I said in shock,
But then I heard a small voice from my pet tree.
He said, "I know I'm grumpy and a bit mean
But wait a while and then you can be keen."

Zara Wall (9)
Worth Primary School, Poynton

The Gobbledegoop In My Back Garden

There's a gobbledegoop in my garden,
Please don't laugh, it's rude to sneer,
It is a real gobbledegoop,
It's really rather queer,
When it first moved to our garden,
Even friends began to talk
It is something to gawp at
With three eyes, one on a stalk.

It's been a living nightmare,
It's eating all our food,
It is a rather graphic beast,
It wanders around completely nude.
I have written this to warn you,
It could save your life today,
If there's a gobbledegoop in your garden
You'd better run away!

Molly Griffith (10)
Worth Primary School, Poynton

I'm An Oreo

I am a biscuit and I would like to say,
I have a white filling and a biscuit on the top,
And also the bottom, black and a bit of white on the eyes,
And also I have a very wide mouth,
I really haven't got eaten yet,
That's a big surprise,
My breath smells like chocolate,
How appetising,
That's how an Oreo rock 'n' rolls,
My ankles go *click click*,
My feet go *bam bam*,
So that's how we live in the packet,
I love the Oreo taste and it might sound strange...
but I'm an Oreo!

Finley Osborne (9)
Worth Primary School, Poynton

Save Our Planet

Let's look after our Earth's beauty
And preserve our wonderful wildlife,
So please save our planet.

Let's save our ice caps from global warming
And save our precious polar bears,
So please save our planet.

Let's save our rainforest from deforestation
And save our outstanding orangutans,
So please save our planet.

Let's save our oceans from litter
And save our superb sea life,
So please save our planet.

So please save our planet
For the generations to come.

Sebastian Davies (10)
Worth Primary School, Poynton

Precious Planet

It's full of greens,
It's full of blues,
And full of colours loved by others.

Our planet's great,
Don't make it a state,
The animals are amazing,
Look at what they're facing.

I love this planet for lots of reasons:
I love the trees,
I love the bees,
I love our school,
I know what you're thinking,
I'm not a fool.

I love our planet, I think it's great,
It's our responsibility
To make it even better.

Harry Roden (10)
Worth Primary School, Poynton

Tennis Champion

Emma Raducanu became a tennis champion
At the age of 16 years old
She did lots of different sports
But tennis stuck out on top for her
She had a very happy childhood
She travelled to a lot of places to do tournaments
Young and old
She was good and kind
She took up tennis at a young age
And she really loves tennis
So she did more of it
And that's how you get better and win
She will play all day
And maybe play all night.
And she never gave up on her goals.

Lucy Francis (10)
Worth Primary School, Poynton

The Golden Goal

The ball looms on the edge of the box
The ball with the number seven
He gets tripped up, the ref blows the whistle
Tweet! It's another free kick
The number seven steps back for the shot
He takes a deep breath
He runs up to it, pow!
Off the right boot into the top corner
Dip, swerve and curve and the net has rippled again
The crowd with a big roar as it goes in
What a goal!
The golden goal!
Perhaps even better!

Kye Hindle (10)
Worth Primary School, Poynton

The Beautiful Rainforest

Hear the rain trickling down the trees,
Feel your hair blowing in the breeze,
Watch the birds fluttering around,
Hear them make a squawking sound,
See the lizard scuttle into the cave,
It's pretty dark in there so it has to be very brave,
At night when the moon rises from behind
the trees,
It dances and prances as it shimmers and gleams,
Now it's time to tuck into bed,
Night, night now, you sleepy heads.

Betsy Joynson (10)
Worth Primary School, Poynton

The Bird And The Mouse

The bird, it's circling,
The mouse looks on,
Can he run?
Can he jolt a log in front?
But the bird may see,
He's too quick for you or me,
The mouse steps out, not seen yet,
Now he takes a risky bet,
And now he's got to make a move,
The bird has seen his chance
In this life-and-death dance

Elliot Murphy-Clarke (10)
Worth Primary School, Poynton

The Spectacular Place Called Space

Welcome to the spectacular place called space,
There's Mercury and Venus, Earth and Mars, Jupiter and Saturn,
Uranus and Neptune and that dwarf planet called Pluto,
Whoosh goes the rocket, zooming past the stars,
The rovers roam around on the surface of the moon,
Shooting stars dance around the sky.

Isaac Dykes (9)
Worth Primary School, Poynton

Rainforests And Jungles

Rainforests and jungles both have trees,
Both have weather,
Both have bees,
Rainforests and jungles like to be loud,
Like to be showered by the wet rain clouds.
Rainforests and jungles hate being chopped,
Hate being burned and left to rot.

Jack Crabtree (10)
Worth Primary School, Poynton

Monster

Rainbow fluff, soft as a pillow,
Gold skin
Nine giant, green and orange eyes
Like lightning, he moves,
Holding a suitcase full of happiness
His voice squeaks, "Come find me..."
We will be friends forever like glue together.

Felicity Longden-Boole (10)
Worth Primary School, Poynton

Space

S uper random place out there
P ops your brain out of the atmosphere
A stronauts swimming out there
C an you see them in the air?
E arth is all the way over there.

Rufus Crank (10)
Worth Primary School, Poynton

Space

S tars everywhere
P lanets galore
A mazing rockets
C olossal comets in an
E ndless void!

Elliot Anderson (10)
Worth Primary School, Poynton

YOUNG WRITERS INFORMATION

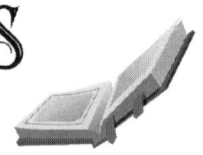

We hope you have enjoyed reading this book – and that you will continue to in the coming years.

If you're the parent or family member of an enthusiastic poet or story writer, do visit our website **www.youngwriters.co.uk/subscribe** and sign up to receive news, competitions, writing challenges and tips, activities and much, much more! There's lots to keep budding writers motivated!

If you would like to order further copies of this book, or any of our other titles, then please give us a call or order via your online account.

Young Writers
Remus House
Coltsfoot Drive
Peterborough
PE2 9BF
(01733) 890066
info@youngwriters.co.uk

YoungWritersUK
YoungWritersCW   **youngwriterscw**

Scan me to watch the Poetry Towers video!